The Best Of

Us

Chapter 1

February 2019, New York City

Thirty minutes ago Alec dreaded attending this corporate launch event, thirty minutes later, he was still here, hoping that someone could make a clone out of him and replace him so he could escape to somewhere he felt more comfortable in, at his own apartment, on his comfy bed or couch, perhaps.

With a glass of wine in his hand, he stood at one corner in his tuxedo that his newly-signed agent, Valentine had chosen for him, praying hard that nobody would recognise him or greet him in any way - he just wanted to stay alone at his very own corner.

He took a sip of the wine and as he looked up through the glass, he saw someone familiar... But it cannot be true... He did a double-take at the person standing just about ten steps away from him.

He was tall, dark, hair so perfectly-styled, smile so charming it could kill. The navy suede suit complimented his skin colour, a big shinny stud on the right side of his ear was too outstanding to be missed but nothing beats those beautiful, big, hazel eyes of his.

It was Magnus, Magnus Bane.

And as he stared at him in complete shock, he realised he had noticed him too and was making his way towards him ever so gracefully, as though he was walking on a beauty pageant's stage with a spotlight shining over him. Insert the signature hand waves and he would have been the winner of that pageant - a result Alec would totally agree with.

He felt his body frozen, his heart beating way out of control, his mind was telling him to run away, again.

Get the fuck out of this fucking event, he could literally hear himself screaming inwardly.

"Alexander Lightwood... What a surprise to see you here," Magnus greeted him with a mega smile.

Really? Magnus? Magnus Bane here in New York? Is this a dream?

"Magnus... What are you doing over here?" He blurted, his eyes unknowingly stopped at the lapel pin that says 'MB' that he was wearing, as though to tell him this was really the Magnus Bane he knew.

"Oh believe me, I'd rather be sipping a cup of tea reading a book or watching TV right now," Magnus chuckled. "But I was forced by my editor to come..." He added, slipping a name card into Alec's hand.

'Magnus Bane, Journalist, New York Weekly'

"Wow... When did this happen? I mean, when did you come back to New York?" Alec had so many more questions in his head but he decided to stick with two, for now.

"A year ago actually, been writing for them... Small magazine but a lot more freedom so I get to choose what I write, well, most of the times," Magnus paused for a while. "How are you doing, the oldest member of the U.S.A swim team?"

"I'm okay I guess..." Alec hated that title and never knew how to respond to it whenever people said it on his face.

This was when Alec saw Lydia walking towards them. She was tall and had an attractive body that made her looked especially stunning in the red dress that she was wearing.

"Hey Alec, I just bumped into my primary school mate... Who is this?" Lydia asked, as soon as she saw Magnus.

"Urm, Lydia, this is Magnus Bane, he was a friend of mine back when I was an exchange student in Australia...

Magnus, this is my girlfriend Lydia Branwell."

There was no way Alec did not notice the utter disappointment written all over Magnus' face once the word 'girlfriend' came out of his mouth. Whether he was disappointed because Alec was now taken, or that Alec was actually seeing a woman would remain a question for later.

"Hey Magnus, what's up?" A man suddenly came in and cut off the conversation.

Thank god for you, Raphael, hallelujah! Magnus could hear himself screaming inside. "Oh Alec, this is Raphael, my boyfriend. Raphael, this is Alexander Lightwood, but you already know that, and his girlfriend Lydia," he said, with a faint smile.

"Ohhh kay... Yes, pleasure Mr. Lightwood, future Mrs. Lightwood. Raphael Santiago," Raphael went ahead to shake both their hands.

There was an awkward silence after that, as though all the words in the world have already been used up, none of them knew what to say next.

"Alec, if you don't mind, I would like to introduce you to my old schoolmate," Lydia was the first to break the silence.

"Oh... Oh... Sure. Gentlemen, excuse me..." Alec said.

Magnus and Raphael gave him a nod as he moved away with Lydia into the party crowd.

About three steps away, Alec turned back to have a peek on Magnus, who was laughing talking to Raphael before they slowly disappeared in the ocean of people as he walked further away.

They looked really good together, he thought.

But what bothered him was the fact that Magnus actually looked better after so many years. If anything, he had definitely aged extremely well and looked much hotter and sexier than the Magnus he first set eyes on three years ago, in a small city down under.

Chapter 2

January 2016, Perth, Western Australia

When Alec found out that Christmas and that the entire winter in the U.S. is actually summer in Australia, he jumped at the opportunity to arrive much earlier before classes started to skip the winter in the States and to enjoy the Aussie sun instead.

On his first weekend in Australia he was already out in a club in the city with some fellow Americans he got to know on the plane. Trained as an athlete since young, his life had been very disciplined with a set of routine - he never was a party person - the time when people go out to party would mean he might already be in bed.

He walked out of the club alone to catch some fresh air. Nighttime in Perth was awfully quiet, he thought. But that was why he chose to come here as an exchange - he wanted a change.

The city looked like what was left after a zombie attack in a movie except a little shop at the corner that saved the day. It was a kebab shop with red and blue neon lights placed at the glass window, calling out for his name and making his stomach growl so he gave in - late night supper once in a while won't kill, he thought.

The shop was tiny and simple but packed with party-goers. He grabbed a kebab and walked out of the shop, found a bench by the road side and sat down, so ready to dig in to his kebab when a figure stood in front of him.

"Excuse me, is this seat taken?"

"Oh no, please... Have a seat..." Alec did not even look up as he took a first bite of the kebab.

"Thank you." The man said as he sat down. "It's a hot day isn't it?"

"Yeah... Hotter in the club..."

"Oh yeah... Also very smokey and way way way too loud, I almost lost my voice trying to tell my mate I was leaving just now... Urggghhh..." The man chuckled, as he too, chucked a big bite of his kebab into his mouth.

"You know, I used to love partying but I guess I'm too old for it now. I'd rather have Clair de Lune playing loudly rather than those songs in the club," the man continued.

"That's the music used in the ending scene of Ocean's 11 series right?" Alec said.

"Yeah! I'm impressed you know!"

"Yeah my sister Izzy... She is a fan of Brad Pitt so I always have to watch with her."

"I'm more of a Matt Damon's fan."

"Oh same!" Alec let out a laugh, too amused that he had found someone who shared so many common interests.

"Oh, I'm Magnus, by the way."

"I'm Alexander, call me Alec..."

As they turned to face one another - the first time the both of them got to see each other properly under the bright street light shining upon their faces, there was an instant spark that they could feel right down in their nerves.

Alec's mesmerising blue eyes were too distracting all Magnus wanted was for time to stop moving so he could just stare into them whole day long. But those well-built broad shoulders of his probably changed his mind about stopping the time as all he wished was to fast-forward everything and fantasising them moving up and down on top of him as they have sex.

Alec too, was in awe of Magnus' big and hazel eyes and that charming smile was too breathtaking. He looked like a prince or an ancient warrior who was out in the jungle, on the way to rescue his princess. Only how he wished he was the princess he was coming for and would plant a kiss on him with his sexy lips.

"Are you... American?" Magnus asked.

"Yea... " Too deep in his fantasy, Alec choked upon saying his first word.

"Are you okay?" Magnus quickly handed his bottle of drinking water to him. "Take some water, it's okay I haven't started drinking it..."

"Thanks..." Alec said as he took a few sips of the water and handed it back to Magnus.

"You keep it, okay?"

"Oh, thanks! I ah... I was saying I'm from New York, but moved to California last year... I ah... Got a swim scholarship in UC..." Alec bit his under lip slightly, a habit that Magnus would later find out it was him being nervous. "Yourself?"

"Oh! I was in New York too until I was 13 when mom and dad decided to move us all back to Indonesia..."

"Oh really? No wonder you sound American too?"

"Oh... G'day mate, you want some Vegemite on your

toastie? Now do I sound Aussie?" Magnus grinned. "I forgot to tell you faking accents is one of my many talents..."

As Alec would learn later, not only Magnus was good at accents, he was also fluent in Indonesian and Mandarin, and was learning Japanese too, which he found very fascinating.

The conversation then went on and on about how Alec had had a surgery on an injured shoulder and had to skip training for a few months, thus missing out on the Olympic Games that year and that was when he decided to do the exchange programme; and that he just arrived a few days ago, still trying to adjust to the slower pace of the city.

Magnus on the other hand, had lived in Perth for the past five and a half year - finishing his business degree and decided to do journalism next and this would be his last semester in Perth before returning home.

The pair ended up chat-chatting for an hour on the bench. There were a lot of laughter as drunk party goers screamed their hearts out on the street, a lot of reminiscing places in New York and sharing of experiences.

They exchanged phone numbers later with a promise to catch up - Magnus insisted that since it was summer and classes haven't started yet it would be perfect timing for him to show him around town.

Chapter 3

February 2019, New York City

"Magnus Bane, Journalist, New York Weekly."

Alec heard himself reciting the same few words in his heart
as he reminisced the times when Magnus announced to
him that he would one day change lives with his words,
touching people or changing laws through his writing.

He had loved watching Magnus immersed in scribbling on
his notepad, sometimes went crazy thinking he had
misplaced his pen which he had actually put it behind his
ear; which had never failed to make him laugh.

He had went online to read some of Magnus' works and
was feeling extremely proud and happy for him, half way
through achieving his dream.

But the last time he saw Magnus, he thought he would
never see him again so it was a huge surprise to see him at
the event few days ago and he had so many question marks
in him that he couldn't help but asked him out for dinner.

Magnus was late, but as he took a seat opposite Alec, loosening his scarf on his neck, Alec saw him dressed in a very nice grey knit sweater with a baby blue shirt inside - he looked too cute and stylish compared to himself - a fitted t-shirt and an army green bomber jacket now hanging over his chair behind him.

"I'm sorry I'm late, just had to wrap up some work," Magnus said, still panting slightly.

"Oh... No, don't worry about it."

As soon as they were done ordering their food, it was Magnus who started the conversation. "So... You must be busy with all the Olympic qualifying events?"

"Yeah... Actually flying off to Russia in two days time for a warm-up event," Alec paused for a few seconds. "Hey... I thought I told you to not look up on me?"

"I did not! I swear! But I'm a journalist and I ought to know a little bit of here and there, even if it means sports news," Magnus put his hands in the air as though he was surrendering a fight or something. "But that's probably why I didn't know you have turned straight and have a girlfriend..." Magnus murmured.

Caught off guard, Alec impulsively bit his lip and immediately regretted it because he knew Magnus knew very well that was a sign of him being nervous.

Like he had just won an one-sided debate, Magnus flipped his hair with his finger. "Well I lied, Raphael isn't my boyfriend, he is just a colleague and he is straight as hell it's a real shame," he chuckled but he had no idea why he found it necessary to explain that to Alec, perhaps he did not want to take away poor Raphael's single status?

"Well... Lydia is still my girlfriend," Alec shrugged.

Magnus said nothing but shot him a sharp glance.

"Urm... What about you? What made you come back to New York?" Alec couldn't believe he had invited Magnus out just for him to press him with question he was too embarrassed to answer.

"Oh my old man passed on a year ago and I was desperate for a change, and the freedom to write... You know how is it working in the media back home. I mean, it's not like it's 100% transparent here too but better, much better," Magnus said while taking a sip of his water.

"I'm sorry about your dad, but I'm really happy for you, to be doing something you've always wanted to do," Alec smiled.

"You're not too bad either... Twenty-six and still swimming your way into the Olympics, you know some people call you an inspiration?"

Alec knew he was blushing listening to the encouraging words from Magnus, like he always did in the past. In fact, it was Magnus who changed his mind about trying for another Olympics. "Ahhh... I feel more like a failure competing against all the younger swimmers only for my first Olympic Games..."

"Alexander... Failure is too big a word. I'm actually so glad that you haven't given up. I believe you can do this, in fact, you know that I have always believe in you."

There was an awkward silence when they both looked straight into each other's eyes, like those eyes were capable of whispering words like 'I miss you' or 'oh how I've miss this, or us'.

Thank goodness for the server as the food arrived sand the mood of the night turned lighter as they started debating if the Pho they were eating were better or the ones that they had back in Perth were better.

As soon as they were done with dinner, Alec offered to drop Magnus home.

"Oh don't worry about it, my place isn't too far away. Besides, you have a girlfriend to go back to, don't you?" Magnus winked at Alec, leaving Alec speechless again.

He stood on the busy street and watched as Magnus walked swiftly away, back facing him, but waving his hand

from far as though he knew Alec was still looking at him,
and slowly disappeared in the crowd.

He remembered vividly, that Magnus had done the same
when he said goodbye to him three years ago.

Chapter 4

July 2016, Perth, Western Australia

In was a wet winter morning, the old wiper swishing on the taxi's windscreen was making awful squeaking sound that was too painful to Magnus' ears.

Rain was splashing on the window, disallowing him to have a proper view of the city before he bid the city a final goodbye. Perhaps, he thought, just perhaps, as cliche as it sounded, the sky was also crying for him and for his departure.

The taxi came to a stop right in front of the airport. Magnus got out, took his luggage, paid the driver and entered the airport.

His huge luggage was heavy - clothes, personal items and books that were with him for a good six years in Australia, some gifts that he had carefully selected to be distributed at home. But nothing was heavier than his heart, leaving behind the city that he had spent the best six years of his life at; and Alec, whom he had just had the most wonderful six months with.

When it all started, he told himself that it might just be a short fling and that separating wouldn't be hurtful. But as time past, and he got to know more about Alec, he just couldn't help falling in love with him. His good look, his vulnerable self amid the huge and tall sportsman figure and all the love and passion that he had unconditionally shared with him - it had all made things tougher when their pre-fixed six month relationship finally drew its final curtain.

Alec had told him it would be too painful to send him off so he had opted not to come. They bid their goodbyes a day before as they went out together to pick gifts for his family and friends in Indonesia, and parted ways at the train station on the way home. Alec did not say a word to him, he simply hugged him and turned away, refusing to even look at him.

It broke his heart to be parted with Alec, but it killed him to see Alec so upset about the farewell that had finally arrived.

He had his luggage checked-in, had one final look at the busy lobby and walked dreadfully towards the immigration check point when he heard someone calling for him from far.

"Magnus! Magnus! Wait!"

He looked into the crowd of people swarming the airport

and saw a very tall figure running frantically, zig-zagging through the crowd, even almost stumbling on someone's luggage. He knew, he knew it was Alec, his Alec was coming for him.

"So... You changed your mind?" Magnus asked, crossing his arms, sounding like he had predicted his appearance, as Alec stopped in front of him, panting and trying to catch some breath.

"Magnus..." Alec stood up straight, pulled Magnus in by his shirt and kissed him.

Magnus gasped, then relaxed his arms, wrapped them around Alec's back and kissed him back. He could hear the crowd around them cheering and clapping like they were watching a movie which ended with someone saying yes to a proposal or a couple finally reunited after a war that tore them apart, or something along the line.

When they finally broke the kiss, Alec refused to let go of Magnus' shirt, squeezing it so tightly in his fist like he was going to tear it off soon. "Promise me one thing, don't contact me, unfollow me on social media so I won't think of you and won't think of us. Let me forget you easier..."

"Really? You came all the way, running like a mad man just to tell me this?" Magnus chuckled, but he couldn't help but felt a lump in his throat as he spoke.

Alec pulled him in again, this time to hug him, one last time as he whispered to Magnus' ear:"I'll miss you, but I will try not to..."

"I'll miss you too, Alexander, and I know you want to forget me, but I won't forget you, I will always remember you, and us," Magnus said.

They held onto each other for a few more seconds as uncontrollable tears came flowing down, wetting their shirts on their shoulders.

As Magnus walked into the immigration check point, he was still sobbing like a baby. He knew, Alec too, was crying watching him from behind. So without looking back, he waved his hand in the air, saying one final goodbye to him.

Chapter 5

March 2019, New York City

"Hey Magnus... Why are you checking out Lydia Branwell?" Clary asked as she saw Magnus' computer monitor filled with pictures of Lydia.

"Just doing some research... Do you know her well?" Magnus asked.

"Well she was a gymnast, not-too-successful I would say... But since retiring she has made a name for herself as a model... She is signed to this company, what's the name... Come let me check for you," Without waiting for Magnus' permission, Clary took over Magnus' computer and started typing.

"Hmmm... Valentine's Management..." Magnus read out the name and was surprised to see Alec's picture right there on the page.

"Hmmm looks like the very hot Alexander Lightwood is their latest recruit! I think they are aiming for good-looking sports personalities... Why are you interested?"

Clary asked.

"Thank you Clary, I'm just you know, curious..."

"Didn't you know Alexander Lightwood?" Raphael came cutting through the conversation, sitting himself on Magnus' desk, right next to his computer.

"You dooooo??? How???" Clary immediately shot a curious glance at Magnus.

"And I haven't forgotten that you owe me one for pretending to be your boyfriend," added Raphael, with a cheeky grin.

"What? Raphael? Your boyfriend?" Clary threw her head back and started laughing.

Magnus rolled his eyes. "First of all, Raphael, it is an absolute honour for you, to be my boyfriend, even if it was for a few seconds. Second of all, why is knowing Alexander Lightwood such a big deal?"

"Well it's not a big deal... Just... If you can, can you get me an autograph? And if he is single, I'm interested???" Clary smiled, fingers now fiddling one of Magnus' pens left on the desk.

"Urghhh... Why is your taste for men so shallow?" Magnus paused for a few seconds, suddenly realising he was also referring to himself. "Well he is taken, apparently, Raphael knows..."

"Yeah... Lydia Branwell... which coincidentally, you guys are checking out right now..."

"Anyway, Clary, didn't you came to say something, or ask me something?" Asked Magnus, trying to change the subject.

"Oh yes, I almost forgot! Congratulations, our beloved editor, Luke wanted me to inform you that you will be in charge of the Pride Month column this coming June! And I'll be your partner in crime... I mean photography!"

"That sounds like great news, I'll talk to you once I have a plan laid out, now shush and get back to your own desks, I have work to do..." Magnus said as he gave them both a weak spank on their asses.

As soon as Clary and Raphael, who are the closest and youngest colleagues of his, left him alone; he couldn't help it anymore, he went on to search for Lydia's Instagram, then Alec's, which he was trying to avoid, religiously adhering to Alec's wish, over the past few years.

A realisation creeped into his mind - for the first few seconds he felt this amusement in him then it turned into disappointment, grief and anger.

If his assumption was right, he felt like all his advices, his encouragements and support, even love for Alec in the past had been so small, so tiny that they had now been all wrapped up in some toilet paper, flushed down into the toilet bowl. Worst, it was Alec who chose to do it, to do it to himself.

This was when his phone let out a vibration. He took his phone up and saw the message.

"Hey Magnus, just came back from Russia, wanna maybe grab a drink tonight?" It was Alec.

Ignored.

A minute later another message came.

"I can pick you up if you want to..."

There were days that Magnus would love to go grab a drink or do many things with Alec. But not today, Alec, definitely not today.

Chapter 6

March 2019, New York City

It was a breezy night in New York.

Alec had finished his training, had a quick and light dinner, drove down to Magnus' office, according to the address on the name card he had given to him earlier. He put on the only jacket he had left in his car, stood himself in front of the office building and waited for Magnus to appear.

The three years they had been apart, Alec had tried his best to focus in his swimming career, trying for his first and last Olympics eappearance. It was in fact Magnus' wish and support that had been pushing him to do so.

He sometimes thought about Magnus and the times they shared together but it didn't bothered him much until he reappeared in his life two weeks ago.

He just couldn't stop thinking about him. He wasn't sure what all these were... They are not together so did that mean they are friends? He had started dating Lydia just about a month ago... Things were more complicated now but he had missed seeing him after less than a week where he was away in Russia so he decided to drop by at his office.

After about fifteen minutes of waiting, Magnus finally jogged out of the building, in his usual stylish work attire, his brown bag hanging on his right shoulder.

Alec's face immediately lit up when he saw him. "Magnus!" He called out.

"What are you doing here?" Asked Magnus.

"Waiting for you... You didn't reply my messages, but you've seen them..." Alec said, simply.

Magnus stood frozen looking at Alec for a while before making his move, walking past him without saying a word to him.

"Hey!" Alec got hold of his arm to stop him.

"What do you want Alexander?" Magnus sounded annoyed.

"What do you mean? I just thought we can catch up..."

"How long have you been dating Lydia? Have you two... Have sex?" Magnus asked, extremely bluntly.

The joy of seeing Magnus again had now gone. The smile
he was wearing while waiting for Magnus had now
vanished. His heart sunk and all he could feel now was
embarrassment and guilt.

"You know what? Don't answer," Magnus started to walk
away again.

For a few seconds, Alec thought of letting Magnus walk
away from him again but he lashed out. "Why do you care
so much anyway? You never cared about anything anyway,
you would just flirt with me, then packed your bags and
went home and that was it... So carefree, like you don't
care, like nothing matters to you, like... Like I don't
matter..."

Even Alec himself was surprised he could have all the
courage to utter those words, the words that he had long
kept to himself.

"Whoa! Look who's talking? Who was the one who asked
me not to contact you and told me in my face that you
wanted to forget me? Do you know how heart-breaking
was it to hear that and then... And then pretend like I was
okay with that?" Infuriated by Alec's non-stop questioning,
Magnus snapped.

"And is that why you are doing something stupid to
yourself? You thought you don't matter and so you've
decided that you don't want to be yourself, turned yourself

straight and date a woman because it would be a great marketing stunt for two good-looking athletes to hook-up and earn big bucks together?"

Alec always knew Magnus was very knowledgable. He once told him that he couldn't help it since he wanted to be a journalist and only hated politics and literature but Why? Why on earth did Magnus just had to know everything? Why did he has to reveal the shame that he was carrying with him?

He stood speechless, now that there was nothing to hide anymore.

"You're disgusting Alexander and you should be ashamed of yourself! And I feel bad for you and your so-called girlfriend," Magnus stormed away without looking back, leaving a stunned Alec on the street.

Chapter 7

January 2016, Perth, Western Australia

After meeting Alec for the first time, Magnus couldn't take him out of his mind. His little smile, curly hair, those innocent yet beautiful blue eyes, and the mysteries behind him that he was so ready to explore.

He liked him a lot but the hunky swimmer appeared to be so vague even his normally accurate gaydar couldn't figure out if he was gay or straight.

In the end, he had decided to bring Alec to the beach on a really hot day. He did some work-out beforehand just to try to impress him but he knew, if Alec try to scan around looking at those girls sunbathing naked, he'll get the hint, he thought.

But soon he'd realised he had asked for too much for a beach day out with Alec when he appeared out of the ocean after a little warm-up and was walking back towards the beach. The scorching sun had made his broad, tanned and glistering shoulders appeared to be extra seductive, he almost wanted to let out a whistle and felt as if his lips were already right there licking his collarbone and fingers caressing that Olympic Games logo tattooed right under it.

Dirty-minded Magnus! Hold on to your horses!!! He had thought to himself.

"Had a good warm-up?" Of course he did not say anything stupid.

"Yeah... It feels pretty good to be back in the water actually..." Alec said as he brushed his wet hair slightly.

"Now look, Australian sun is no joke... Would you mind?" Magnus threw a bottle of sunscreen into Alec's hand and laid himself on the sheet, back facing Alec.

Alec was left helpless as he held on to the bottle of sunscreen. He felt strange and awkward and for a second he wanted to say no but there was no harm just helping applying some sunscreen onto someone's back, maybe?

He popped open the bottle and started rubbing Magnus' back awkwardly with the sunscreen. Somehow, touching Magnus' skin like that sent shivers to his body, in a good way that he never expected it to be.

Magnus on the other hand, without Alec seeing it, had a mischievous smirk on his face.

After a few seconds, Magnus got up and took over the

bottle of sunscreen.

"Alright, thanks, now let me help you too, Aussie sun is super dangerous..." Magnus said, as he gently laid his palm on Alec's arm.

Taken by surprise, Alec flinched, flipping Magnus' hand away, causing him to drop the sunscreen onto the sand.

Taken aback, Magnus rolled his eyes. "You know, it's not contagious."

"What?"

"I said, it's not contagious. Me, being gay isn't contagious."

By then Magnus had had enough. Maybe Alec is straight, even if he isn't; he would be few thousand feet deep in his closet and he wouldn't want to, also not interested, in any way, out him.

Chapter 8

January 2016, Perth, Western Australia

Alec knew he had unintentionally offended Magnus but he couldn't bring himself to say anything to him so they stayed silent throughout the entire train ride back to the city before he finally found the courage to talk to him again.

"Magnus... I'm sorry... I didn't mean to..." Alec stuttered, biting his lip.

"It's alright, I'm quite used to it," Magnus answered, simply.

"Let me buy you dinner, or a drink to make it up," Alec suggested.

Magnus accepted the offer, led Alec to a Chinese restaurant in Chinatown, expecting the dinner to be filled with ghost of silence.

But as soon as Alec had his first bottle of beer down, the situated started to change.

"Nobody knows I'm gay. They cannot know I'm gay or they'll disown me... You know what I mean?"

Startled by how event had just taken a huge turn from the beach day out to the dinner table, Magnus was more amused by Alec's concern about people disowning him. "I don't get it... You are so lucky to live in a country where gay marriage is already legal while I have to pretend to be someone else back home because I could be punished in public for maybe just holding a man's hand," Magnus sighed.

"Do you know the one thing I've enjoyed the most living over here is the fact that people here are more open-minded, less judgmental when I want to wear whatever I like and be comfortable in my own skin?"

"I don't know Magnus, it's just it's terrifying to come out to a family who have been religiously going to church every Sunday..."

"Come on, what era are we living in Alec? Everyone is talking about being proud of who you are and be unapologetically yourself. I'm sure even your family knows they are not living in some history books. Give some respect to the people who had fought for people like us..." Magnus was starting to feel like he was preaching and he wasn't even sure if Alec was sober enough to take in all his words.

"I guess I'm just such a chicken," Alec shrugged.

"Why are you so scared of everything anyway? I saw you swimming just now and your shoulder looks perfectly fine to me, why are you skipping training?"

Alec was surprised at how Magnus was able to see through all the secrets that he once thought only he himself knew. "The injury means I'll miss qualifying for the Olympics and I think that's the end of my swimming career... I'll be freaking 27 years old at the next Olympics..."

"Oh now you are trying to make me feel ancient aren't you? I'm turning 27 and I'm still studying, I'm such a failure, aren't I?" Magnus rolled his eyes.

Alec could only gave him a weak smile and that was all he could remember of the night as he gulped down more beer after dinner and had probably talked more than he usually does.

The next thing he knew, he woke up with a mild headache in an unfamiliar-looking room. He was alone on a single bed with a blanket over him, still wondering where the hell was he at until he flipped to see a figure lying on the floor, next to the bed.

It was Magnus and it reminded him that he had probably ended up too drunk and Magnus had to bring him back to his place and had given up his bed for him while he slept on the floor, all curled up like a shrimp, shivering slightly without any cover.

He got down extremely carefully, put the blanket over him and couldn't help but took the opportunity to stare at a sleeping Magnus - now hair all ruined, but so handsome still, even in his sleep. He could even feel his heart beating faster, face heating up just looking at him like that.

Suddenly a hand came out of nowhere and grabbed his wrist. "You have been staring at me for a while now, is there anything I can help with?" Magnus said with a smirk, eyes still shut.

Shocked, Alec stumbled and fell on the already cramped space, landing on one of Magnus' legs as he let out a groan.

All he remembered after that was apologising to Magnus and ran out of his room clumsily, then the apartment, leaving with curious eyes from his housemates sitting in the living room staring at him.

Chapter 9

March 2019, New York City

It was a Friday night, Alec had just wrapped up his last training of the week and found himself in an old, quiet pub - the only pub in New York that he would go to occasionally whenever he needed some time off.

It was also where he had a meeting with Valentine two months ago where he convinced him that he will help him in getting sponsors if he make it to the Olympic Games next year and a fantastic post-swimmer career in modelling, TV or films, whichever tickles his fancy. He knew he would be too shy for any of those but Valentine assured him that that was going to be his best asset. "People loves someone who is shy, they think it's cute and feel relatable!" He said.

Then Valentine dropped him a bombshell - he wanted him to 'try' dating one of his girls under his management - Lydia Branwell.

"Well she had a mediocre sportswoman career but she is gorgeous and intelligent, and trying to make a name as a model and you two should be together and help each other out."

"You two looked perfect together - both super good-looking and I foresee I can sell you two as inspirations to others who are still going strong in a second career after retiring from sports. I can imagine so many opportunities for you two as a couple, rather than you or her, individually," Valentine had told Alec.

Alec and Lydia hit it off right away - coming from a sport background helped built the bonds between them but when it came to intimacy, Alec just couldn't bring himself to do it, telling her he wasn't ready.

Lydia wasn't stupid either, she knew something was amiss but she also knew very well that she needed Alec to be with him if she wanted more publicity. "We are staying together until nobody cares about us," she said to Alec.

Alec's mind was all clouded with the thought of what Magnus had said to him few days ago but he knew everything Magnus said about him was right. He was disgusting and should be ashamed of himself for doing things that are not true to himself, and for not being able to come out yet after so many years.

The fears he had in him never left him, especially after Magnus and him parted, he felt like the biggest support system that he had was gone - nobody was there to tell him everything was going to be okay, or say things like "I will be here for you no matter what happen".

Perhaps all he needed was Magnus back in his life, but it wasn't the encouragement and support from him that he needed because he knew very clearly, since the night he saw him at the event, that he still had feelings for him.

After a few pints of beer, he knew he was unfit to drive home so he took out his phone and started to look for someone to call for help.

Jace, the teammate? Isabelle, the sister?

He made the call.

"Yes Alexander, what do you want?"

It was Magnus that he had called.

"Oh Magnus, oh my god, I'm sorry I didn't mean to call you but okay... What do I want? I want you..." He chuckled.

"Oh god... You are drunk again... You should know your booze tolerance isn't that good right?" Magnus sighed on the other end of the phone.

"Well my tolerance for you isn't that good either..." At that point Alec was almost just mumbling all by himself.

"Damn it Alec, where the hell are you?"

"Me? I'm... I wanna be in you! Do you wanna be in me?"
Alec let out a laugh.

The next thing he remembered he was already out of the
pub, throwing up near a an alley next to the pub when
someone came, one hand stroking his back, the other
holding onto his arm helping him to stand properly.

"Urgghhh gross... What did you just eat for dinner?"

Chapter 10

February 2016, Perth, Western Australia

Summer was almost coming to an end when classes started for most students in Australian universities.

Alec just attended a welcoming party for international students and just settled himself with his laptop in a sad corner of the library, checking for new emails from home.

Alec had not seen Magnus since the embarrassing morning where he woke up on Magnus' bed in his apartment after having a little too much drinks a night before. He thought he must have appeared to be such a freak or a weirdo for staring at Magnus and then just ran out on him right after.

It felt so strange to him that he was so cautious about how Magnus would think about him. It was even stranger that he actually felt like he was missing Magnus, it was like a feeling that he had never felt before for anybody. He wanted to know how was he doing? Was he very busy? Has he ever wondered what happened to him after that morning?

"Excuse me, is this seat taken?" As he was deep in his own thought, a familiar voice came.

"Ah... No..."

He looked up as Magnus sat himself down ever so nonchalantly right opposite him, dropped his bag on the ground, took out his books and notepad, immersed into whatever he was reading and scribbling.

Magnus appearing out of nowhere messed Alec's mind a bit he almost forgot what was he doing here in the library. Oh yes, he was supposed to be checking his mailbox but he couldn't help but to look up to check on Magnus. He loved how serious and cute he looked when he was hard at work, even the sound of him writing frantically on the paper sounded like Beethoven or Mozart to him.

Then suddenly he felt something brushing his shin under the table, the movements were gentle and frequent, and he knew it was done intentionally to get his attention.

Magnus left out a sighed. "You know it's quite rude to ALWAYS stare at people like that?" Magnus said, without even looking up.

Again, Alec panicked.

"I... I'm getting a drink from the vending machine..." He stuttered and ran away.

He ran to a corner of a book shelf, sat himself down on the ground and calm himself down. His heart was pounding in an uneasy pace and he felt like cold sweet were coming out of him. He couldn't handle Magnus with such brazen attitude yet some part of him actually loved how flirty he was with him.

He must have disappeared from the table for way too long when Magnus found him sitting at the corner.

"There you are... I thought you were getting a drink?" He said, while sitting himself down besides him.

Alec, struggling to find words to say decided to apologise. "I'm sorry..."

"Oh, for what?" Magnus asked.

"For... For..."

"For being gay? Or for being extremely scared of me? Am I that scary?" Magnus chuckled.

"Are you always so flirty?" Alec asked.

"Really? You find that flirty?" Magnus smiled and shook his head. "Then you have seen nothing yet..."

"Is it possible that you can stay back over here or move back to the States after you finish your study?" Alec asked abruptly.

"I told you I've spent all my dad's money doing two degrees here, and they are old, they need me to be home... Why? Is that bothering you?"

"Yes..."

Magnus raised an eye brow looking at him, waiting for him to continue.

"Because I like you and I don't want you to leave," Alec blurted, so out-of-the-blue even he himself was surprised.

"You do?" Magnus actually did not sound surprise at all. He edged closer to Alec, and without any alert, planted a kiss on him, feeling his soft and warm lips for the first time. Well you know what, I like you too, like a lot," Magnus whispered, mouth still extremely close to Alec he could feel his breathing.

The kiss triggered Alec to go for more as he went on to cup Magnus' cheeks, mouth capturing Magnus' and kissed him again. Magnus hummed in approval and kissed him back passionately.

When they finally broke the kiss, Magnus reached his hand behind Alec's head and fished out a book from the shelf.

"The Catcher in the Rye," he read out the title of the book.

"Interesting choice Alexander... Although a little sick and weird to commemorate a first kiss..." he grinned.

"Sick and weird? Do you think I'm sick and weird too?" Alec asked.

"You?" Magnus chuckled. "No, far from it... You're precious, very precious."

Chapter 11

March 2019, New York City

Alec felt like he just had a very bad nightmare as he woke up in shock, squinted his eyes to the brightness of the few strands of sunlight shining through the gaps of the curtain. He let out a loud groan and peeled open his eyes slowly to realise he was alone, on a bed and in a room that was not his.

He scanned the room briefly but did not have enough time to figure out where he was before the door knob turned and Magnus walked in, dressed in a sweat-soaked sport attire, obviously just came back from a jog or some exercise session.

"Alec... How are you feeling?" Magnus asked, looking concerned, as he sat down by his side on the bed.

Alec slowly sat himself up, shook his head and winced. "Just the head feeling really heavy..."

Magnus rubbed his thigh gently through the blanket, moved himself closer, planted a kiss on his temple, then moved away. "See if I could kiss away the pain..."

Alec shut his eyes as he enjoyed the moment, then a tiny grin appeared on his face. "Just like the song?"

"Just like the song..." Magnus replied.

"I can be your hero baby... I can kiss away the pain..." Alec started singing, making Magnus smiled extremely sweetly.

"Okay you just let out a bad puke breath," Magnus said.

Alec immediately shut his mouth with his hand as he suddenly realised this must have been Magnus' room and that he had spent a night here.

He watched as Magnus walked to his wardrobe, undressed himself and put on a fresh shirt.

Even in that short few seconds of time, Alec could see Magnus' dark, toned, muscular body - now almost looked like it was sprinkled with glitter, with drops of sweat all over it. He has always envied his darker skin but Magnus' body, although not as well-built as his swimmer body, was looking better than the last time he've seen it three years ago. Magnus must have been working on those abs a lot, he thought.

"Magnus... What happened last night?" He asked.

"You seriously don't remember anything, don't you?"

"I remember drinking... Maybe a bit too much?"

"Maybe? I thought you athletes have some kinda strict diet and alcohol shouldn't be part of it?" Magnus asked.

"Anyway, then you called me, said a lot of things... You really should watch out the amount of alcohol you are drinking cos a drunk, talkative Alec is really unbearable," Magnus chuckled. "Well I think a too quiet and too shy Alec is unbearable too..." He mumbled.

"Oh god... What did I say?"

"Urm... Mostly horny and cheesy stuff... Something about wanting to be in me..." Magnus shrugged, but Alec could see him turning red a little.

He covered his face with his hands in embarrassment. "Damn... I'm so sorry Magnus... And thank you for taking me home... Did we do something... On your bed?" Out of nervousness, Alec moved his gaze around the room while asking the question, avoiding direct eye contact with Magnus.

"Don't be silly... I slept on the couch the whole night, it's a good thing I bought quite a good quality couch... Anyway, come out, I've got us some sandwiches, then you can take some painkillers cos Enrique Iglesias is a liar and you shouldn't believe in romantic songs like that," Magnus said, still smiling.

Alec stood up, trailed behind Magnus as they walked out of the room as he realised all these were too good to be true.

Was he in a dream? Didn't they just sort of had an argument earlier? Why is Magnus being so sweet and nice to him now?

Like his room, the apartment was tidy and simple, everything felt like it was all very temporary - it reminded him of Magnus' single bedroom that he had rented back in Perth that he had spent a lot of time in.

As Magnus walked to the kitchen and started pouring them some coffee, Alec, still massaging his temple, wandered around and saw a big book shelf filled with books - probably the only thing that felt like it had been there for years. But it was undoubtedly Magnus' because reading was his favourite and he has always prefer holding a book than any gadgets in his hands.

He strolled past the book shelf and realised the middle shelf was the only one not fully filled yet. He bend down and realised the first one was The Catcher in the Rye, the next one was also The Catcher in the Rye but with a different cover design. Then the next one another design, then there were some more in some foreign languages that he did not understand, same as the next few ones. He couldn't help but took out some of them and realised they were all probably the same book, only all in different languages because he could see the author name was the same - J.D. Salinger.

Has Magnus been trying to gather all versions of The Catcher in the Rye?

Chapter 12

March 2019, New York City

"Yes Alec, I've been collecting them, The Catcher in the Rye in different languages, and different editions," Knowing it was now too late to hide, Magnus admitted, as he placed two mugs on the dining table and sat down.

"But why?" He asked as he walked slowly towards the table.

"Because... Oh you know why..." Magnus murmured, quickly unwrapped the sandwich and passed it over to Alec.

"I still have the one that you gave me, it's in my parents' place," Alec said.

"Well, good to know..."

As the pair started eating their breakfast, it became clear that the atmosphere was getting a little awkward with the both of them eating silently, not looking up at each other.

As Alec finished his sandwich, took the pills that Magnus had left on the table for him and started sipping his coffee, he decided to break the silence.

"I wouldn't have thought that the book means so much to you..." He said.

Magnus stayed silent for a few seconds, trying to find the right words to explain things. "Alexander... While you were trying to forget me... Or us, I was trying to preserve the memories as much as possible. I mean, it was special, you were special to me..."

"And... Even though we are not together anymore, it doesn't mean I don't care for you. Not contacting you doesn't mean I have not been reading the news and I have been hoping and praying for the best for you. Even until today I will still say I care for you a lot, in fact I don't think I'll ever stop caring for you... Which was probably why I was so pissed off the other day and I'm sorry if I was too harsh on you."

Magnus' sudden confession had left Alec speechless. All along he had always assumed that Magnus' flirty and outgoing demeanour meant he would forget about them and would have moved on with life easily and would probably be with another guy, or a few guys in fact by now. He always thought that 'Alexander Lightwood' would ended up simply as one of his many flings that he would have written about if he ever had a dating history book or was going to publish a book about it. "Magnus... I... I had no idea..."

"That's alright... Anyway, what's over is..."

"Magnus, I miss you, I miss us..." Alec blurted.

"I know..."

"You know?" Alec raised his eye brows.

"You know you often only tell the very truth when you are drunk..." Magnus was certainly referring to him coming out to him the last time he was drunk.

"Did I tell you I miss you?"

"Among other things, yes..."

Before Magnus could finish his sentence, Alec had already pulled him in by his shirt, locked their lips and started kissing him - taking in the lingering taste of coffee left on his lips, but most importantly, the lips that he had missed kissing for three whole years.

Magnus gasped slightly and hesitated at first, then decided to kiss him back. But slowly he found an uncertainty hanging in the kiss that he had responded with.

"You should probably go," Magnus said, as he pulled

himself away, eyes still staring into Alec's blue eyes.

"But I don't want to..." Alec couldn't help but pouted, he knew at that moment, all he wanted was Magnus, Magnus back in his life again.

"We can't go on like this... I don't want to be an affair to your relationship with someone else. Plus it's a Saturday Alexander, don't you have your Saturday family lunch to go to?"

"Oh shit... What time is it?" Alec checked his phone and knew he was going to be late to see his parents and sister. Then it hit him that Magnus remembered the Saturday family lunch tradition that he had once told him before. "Magnus... You actually remember that?"

"Alexander, I remember everything... Your lactose intolerance, which was why your coffee was black just now. And you didn't actually tell me where were you last night but you've told me three years ago about the only pub you would go to for drinks in New York..." Magnus shrugged.

Alec was beaming from ear-to-ear now, like a schoolboy finding out about his crush also having feelings for him. The fact that Magnus had remembered and was even trying to preserve all the details that he had shared with him before, melted him a little, or maybe a lot.

"Come on, I'll call you an Uber to the pub to get your car."

Magnus said as he handed Alec's jacket back to him.

"Magnus, thank you," Alec went ahead and gave him a peck on the cheek this time, before rushing off.

Chapter 13

March 2016, Perth, Western Australia

As a new couple, Alec and Magnus spent a lot of their class-free times at an Olympic sized swimming pool near the city and then at Magnus' room in an apartment he share-rented with a fellow Indonesian and a Chinese housemates.

Magnus would sit or walk besides the pool as he watched and timed Alec's swim, sometimes shouting words of encouragement from the side like an angry personal trainer. Alec was amused by the shouting at first, always trying to hold a straight face, but he knew Magnus was just pushing him to work harder. And the fact that he felt stronger day by day made him realised how important Magnus' supports was to him.

It was another swim day done and they were in Magnus' place again - Magnus sitting on his bed, back leaning against the wall, Alec rested his head on his lap when Magnus decided to show him how he looked like as a high school kid back in Indonesia.

"No way... This can't be you..." Alec lunged out and grabbed Magnus' phone.

It was quite a different Magnus - much chubbier, thick glasses over his eyes and the awkward smile he was wearing on his face was more like Alec's than his.

"Well, that was me... Always being bullied in school, even relatives, for being chubby and flamboyant..."

There was a sense of sadness and helplessness in Magnus' voice as he spoke about his past and it was the first time Alec caught a glimpse of a different person in Magnus - the vulnerable part of him that he was very glad to be introduced to.

"You looked different, but it was still you, I can see it, still very handsome... Also, nobody would bully you if they see you now... Or read what you write!" Alec flapped the papers that he was helping Magnus to proof-read.

"Oh that is only for my Critical Thinking assignment, that isn't really any real news article writing..."

"Well I'm not too sure about the subject matter, but your writing, the use of words are extraordinary... You are really gifted Magnus and you should really stick to writing."

"Really? You really think so?"

"Yeah... I mean it, you are seriously talented... you're such a gem, how did I find you?"

"Well maybe it was me who found my way to you? The way you swam just now... I would die to swim like that, or even just half as good as you... You're the real gem..." Magnus said, as he stroked Alec's hair.

"Either way..." Alec got up and sat on Magnus' lap, cupped his cheeks with his hands and started kissing him.

They knew, in their hearts, that that was the prelude that promised something more than just a passionate kiss.

Magnus returned the kiss hard he almost tasted blood, his hands scooping Alec's ass and pushed him in closer to him, feeling his body and awakening every desire in his body. They could feel each other's heartbeats now through the wall of their chests, as adrenaline ran higher and the kiss became messier.

They broke the kiss; but hands still holding onto each other tightly, eyes staring into each other's so intensely, breathing slightly faster, but said no words as they started stripping off each other's t-shirts.

"Wait..." Magnus whispered.

He pushed Alec away and went to his desk and reached for his laptop, turned on Clair de Lune, adjusted the volume of his speakers to the maximum, took off his shorts and went back to the bed, pushed Alec down and went on top of him.

As the overtune of the famous classical music started playing, he started kissing Alec's forehead, his eyes, his nose, then his lips. Slowly, he moved down to his neck and collarbone, causing Alec to moan a little too loud.

"Shhh... Not too loud..." Magnus whispered, not wanting his housemates to hear some free show.

The pair giggled a little at each other's faces as they picked up where they had left earlier.

They progressed almost fully following the rhythm of Clair de Lune - slow and gentle at the beginning, then rough and desperate when the music reached its climax.

They knew it wasn't a perfect first time as they could only pray that the music was loud enough to cover their already-controlled excitement, as well as the creaking sound the poor old bedspring was letting out as they allowed themselves to explore each other's bodies - moving ever so carefully, trying not fall off the limited space given it was only a single bed. But it was perfect in many other ways because it felt real and it felt right.

Chapter 14

March 2016, Perth, Western Australia

As they finished, Magnus and Alec laid naked and extremely close to each other on Magnus' very small single bed.

Alec had his head planted in Magnus' neck, feeling his beautiful skin and breathing that cooling down now, his long legs were curling up onto Magnus' legs. Magnus was also cradling him against his body with one arm over his broad shoulder, fingers twirling Alec's curly hair and sniffing them - which now had a mixture of smells from sweat, chlorine and his chamomile-scented shampoo that Alec had just used in the shower earlier.

Clair de Lune was still playing on repeat in the background, but in a softer volume now, like a lullaby that was meant to put a baby to sleep.

"Magnus, this is a mistake," Alec said, almost too suddenly.

Magnus snorted. "Oh my god Alexander... That's not

exactly a very nice thing to say to someone whom you just had séx with..."

"But it is... What am I supposed to do when you go home in July?"

Magnus went silent.

"What have we done? We have started something that will definitely end in a tragedy... There is no happy ending to this!"

Magnus let out a laugh. "Tragedy? Oh don't you be over-dramatic..." There was a long pause before he continued. "You know what would be a mistake? What would be a tragedy?"

"What?" Alec asked, as he moved himself up, eyes looking straight into Magnus' so fondly, waiting for an answer.

"It would be a tragedy if you didn't tell me you prefer boys, or never told me how you feel about me..." Magnus said, as he brushed Alec's cheekbones lovingly with his fingers.

Alec looked at him and smiled. "Who wouldn't fall for you..." He said.

Magnus turned red to Alec's words as Alec smiled again looking at how cute he was being so shy.

Magnus then let out a sigh. "Alexander... I know that we may not go beyond this six months, but that is why we need to saviour every second together, or every moment like this... Or it will be a real tragedy... And I don't know about you but I know I will regret it one day when I grow older, like when I'm 80 and think about that beautiful boy who was never meant to be, whom I've never kissed, whom I've never held his hands, whom I've never make love with."

"And... We don't know what our future holds right? Maybe somewhere, some time, we may meet each other again?" By now, Magnus had reached a hand down to hold Alec's hand and put them in between their chests. "I don't know Alexander... Just let me, let us enjoy what we have now okay?"

Alec gave him a weak smile. He knew in some ways Magnus was right, but he couldn't help but thought about the fact that their days together were numbered and that he dared not count them at all, fearing the devastation it will bring to him to see Magnus go.

He moved his face closer to Magnus, cupped his cheeks and kissed him. He will never get sick of kissing Magnus, he thought to himself.

Chapter 15

April 2019, New York City

"Break a leg!"

Magnus' message to Alec before he flew to Italy for the first Olympics qualifying event was so simple but it made him so happy. In fact, he felt like he hadn't been so happy for a very long time now until the Saturday morning at Magnus' apartment.

He had failed in his first attempt to win a place in the Olympics but surprisingly, he was not as stressed nor was he too disappointed about the result. In fact, he had swam one of his personal best time in Italy and it was very close to the time needed to beat some of his competitors. He'd like to think that it was all Magnus' motivation that had helped him achieved that. In fact, it was Magnus all along, who had encouraged him to not quit chasing his Olympics dream since day one.

He was feeling very confident of doing better and finally securing a spot in next year's Olympic Games at the following tournament that was coming up in another month time in South Korea.

The trip to Italy also allowed him to have some alone time to think through a lot of things and he had returned home with a clearer mind and a mission - to make everything right and to fix the mess that he had created for himself.

He kept thinking about the wonderful Saturday morning spent at Magnus' where he knew for sure there was clearly still something between Magnus and him after so many years. At least he was clear of his feelings for him and there was glimpse of hope that Magnus feel the same for him.

As badly as he wanted to win that Olympics ticket, he was also determined to win Magnus back. He had a plan, he sent out a message, made some appointments, changed some plans and was on his way to Magnus' apartment.

It was a Sunday close to Magnus' birthday, as he arrived in front of Magnus' apartment building right before the clock hit 7am and waited for Magnus to appear. And there he was, as predicted, in his sport attire again, ready to jog out of the building.

He honked for Magnus' attention as he winded down his window.

Magnus, who wasn't sure who was it in the car, walked cautiously towards the car and bend himself down to find

Alec in the car.

"What are you doing here?" Magnus asked, raising an eye brow.

"Hey birthday boy... Care to give up a weekend work-out to go for an early birthday brunch?" Alec asked.

"My birthday isn't until Thursday..."

"Which you will be working and I will be training, and you might have loads of plans with your friends or colleagues, so... I'm asking you again, care to go get some birthday brunch?"

Magnus threw his head up, rolling his eyes a little and crossed his arms. "Do I have a choice?"

"Not really..." Alec chuckled.

"Do I get to change first?"

"No... You look fine, it's a casual brunch not a fine-dining dinner, come on, let's go!"

Although a little reluctant, Magnus finally gave in and hopped onto Alec's car as they took off.

Chapter 16

April 2019, New York City

It was quite a long drive before they arrived at their destination.

Turned out Alec had brought Magnus to a hidden warehouse-turned-cafe that was located within an industrial area in the city. It was spacious, but very tastefully decorated with vintage and rugged furnitures; and old movie posters hanging all over the wall. There was even an old-school jukebox blasting out oldies when they arrived.

As they walked through the entrance and took in the ambiance, Magnus immediately fell in love with the place and knew Alec had picked the cafe simply because he knew he will like the vibes. They found a table and sat down, Magnus was already moving his shoulders slightly to the music playing from the jukebox when he saw that the drink menu had 'Flat White'.

"Oh do you know it isn't easy to find Flat White here?" He said.

"I know... And that was why I had to bring you here, I've done my research," Alec grinned.

Magnus returned with a smile - one that Alec was very glad to see. It was sweet and assuring that he liked this place, he liked his birthday surprise and that it was a great start to the day.

Nailed it, Alec, he thought to himself.

Later, as they enjoyed their food and coffee, Magnus told Alec about his plan for his column for the coming Pride Month.

"So I've got an Oscar-nominated film director who have made some of the best movies, I'm such a big fan and I can't tell you how excited I was when he agreed to be interviewed!" Magnus said, as he sent a forkful of croissant into his mouth.

"You sure are excited... So excited you have croissant crumbs all over your mouth..." Alec chuckled.

"Is it?" Magnus tried to clean himself with his fingers.

"Come, let me help you..." Alec said, as he took a serviette and went ahead to help Magnus brushed away the crumbs sticking around his mouth.

"Thank you..." Magnus said, feeling a little awkward as he

looked up at Alec, who was also staring at him in adoration.

The two looked at each other for a few seconds and felt all the emotions and memories rushing back into their heads. It felt like the first time they have met each other's eyes outside that dodgy Kebab shop on that beautiful summer night in Perth where there were instant sparks in the first stare they had.

Feeling a little awkward, Magnus moved his gaze away, taking a sip of his coffee. "Their Flat White is not too bad at all!" He announced as he smiled over his cup.

"Magnus, I'm really happy for you..."

"Hey listen..." Magnus had stopped Alec from finishing his sentence when he heard the song that was playing from the jukebox.

"What's that?"

"Shhh..."

It was Let's Groove by Earth, Wind and Fire playing.

"That's our song!" Magnus exclaimed, beaming from ear-to-ear.

As the song played further, Alec slowly recognised the

song, it was one of the songs they used to listen to when they were back in Perth. He smiled in response before watching Magnus stood up from his seat and started dancing to the song by the side of the table.

"Come on Alec, dance with me..." Magnus said.

"No... No way..." Alec started waving his hands frantically.

"Oh come on, it's my birthday treat right? So I get to demand for something?"

Alec couldn't say no anymore to that as he stood up embarrassingly and started moving his body awkwardly opposite Magnus.

Few seconds later a few other patrons and even some of the staffs of the cafe started to join in the dance too as the two of them giggled and danced their way through the song. It wasn't even proper dancing, just a lot of random and weird swinging, shaking, twirling and wiggling but they were having a ball doing it.

There were an applause when the chorus of the song ended and they decided to stop dancing. Magnus held Alec's hand and took a bow, like they have just finished a performance on stage.

"Oh that was fun..." Magnus said, panting slightly from the dancing.

Alec couldn't help but smiled in agreement over what just happened. It was ridiculously crazy to dance in a cafe but somehow it felt good to let himself loose, doing crazy thing like that, especially with Magnus, he thought.

He gulped down some coffee and asked Magnus:"Do you have any plan later?"

"Not really... Why?"

"You'll see..." Alec replied with a smirk on his face.

Chapter 17

April 2015, Margaret River, Western Australia

Autumn that year in Perth was horrible. Rain was pouring almost every day like the sun was taking its winter nap and it was impossible to move around the city without ending up soaking wet.

So when the weather forecast had indicated that it would be a beautiful sunny weekend, Magnus had rented a car and drove Alec and himself out to the state's famous vineyard just for a little getaway - where they could be themselves, just the two of them, not spending time in his tiny single bedroom.

The drive itself was too fun to forget as they grooved cheekily to the music, sang along the songs that were blasting through the player, from faking a falsetto to The Sylistic, Earth, Wind and Fire and The Bee Gees, to belting out cheesy 90s boy band tracks that they both agreed were 'so bad yet so good'.

They may be three years apart in terms of age difference and had came from different cultural backgrounds, both had very different personalities, yet somehow in many ways, they spoke the same language, shared the same sentiment for many things like music, movies and anything pop culture.

As they settled at the accommodation that they've booked, seeing the sun was still shining brightly, Magnus quickly put out a large sheet on the grass outside. Autumn was the end of grapes season at the vineyard and the scenery was breathtakingly beautiful. It was also extremely quiet, with only soft bird chirping from afar can be heard.

Magnus laid himself down on his belly, covered himself with a thin blanket, passed one to Alec and started to read his book, while scribbling down notes on a notepad besides him. Alec found comfort laying on Magnus' back, with his sunglasses on and staring into the blue sky, covering his ears with headphones as the two of them enjoyed a beautiful afternoon under a sunny autumn day.

It must have been at least half an hour later when Magnus started to wiggle his body, signalling Alec that he was going to get up. Alec moved, sat legs-crossed, as Magnus did the same sitting right across him.

"What are you listening to?" Magnus asked, knocking on his headphones lightly with the back of his finger.

Alec removed his headphones, put it over Magnus's head gently. "Listen," he said, almost too softly, with a smile.

"Oh my god, this is going to be so cheesy..." Magnus
giggled as he heard the beginning of the song by no other
than the Backstreet Boys, Alec must have been continuing
the boy bands songs obsession since the drive a while ago.

"Shhh... Listen," Alec had put his finger over Magnus' lips
to stop him from talking.

'Remember when
Never needed each other
The best of friends
Like sister and brother
We understood
We'd never be alone

Those days are gone
Now I want you so much
The night is long
And I need your touch
Don't know what to say
Never meant to feel this way
Don't want to be
Alone tonight

What can I do to make you mine?
Falling so hard, so fast, this time
What did I say?
What did you do?
How did I fall in love with you?

I hear your voice
And I start to tremble
Brings back the child that
I resemble
I cannot pretend
That we can still be friends
Don't want to be
Alone tonight

What can I do to make you mine?
Falling so hard, so fast, this time
What did I say?
What did you do?
How did I fall in love with you?'

As the song played through the headphones, Magnus realised that the lyrics were truly words that Alec wanted to dedicate to him. The words made his heart squeeze in sorrow. He moved the headphones down to his neck, looked up at Alec, who had been staring at him lovingly for the past minutes, took one of his hands up and kissed it on his knuckles as he felt tears welling up in his eyes.

The ray of sunlight came just in time then, shining onto his face and created a rainbow on the tears that came running down his cheeks.

Alec brushes the tears off with the back of his fingers as he couldn't hold on to his own tears as well.

"I love you Alexander."

"I love you too Magnus."

There was a mournful silence after that, as though the entire place, or the whole world around them, as they would have imagined, knew how insanely in love they both were, too hard and too fast, just like how it was sang in the song. But worst, the time they had together was entering a painful countdown.

Chapter 18

April 2019, New York City

It was already late afternoon when they wrapped up their brunch date as Alec brought Magnus back to his apartment, opened the fridge, took out a bottle of red wine, a little box and placed them on the dining table.

Magnus was sitting on a chair scanning around the apartment as Alec poured them some wine and opened the box that had a slice of cake in it.

"I know you don't fancy cake but a slice for a special occasion won't hurt right?" Alec said.

Magnus nodded with a smile.

"Happy Birthday, Magnus..." Alec said as he raised his glass of wine and heard it clang with Magnus' glass.

"Thank you, Alexander..."

They both took a sip of the wine as they eyed over each other over the rim of the glasses.

"You know I actually wanted to bring you to a local vineyard but when I checked they were booked for a wedding so I thought if I can't bring you to a vineyard, I could bring the vineyard to you here..." Alec said, looking very proud with what he had planned.

"Well A plus for the effort!" Magnus replied.

"I think we could do better!" Alec grabbed his phone and started scrolling for a few seconds before turning on a song.

As the intro of the song started playing, Magnus immediately knew what song it was.

Alec stood up and put his hand out to Magnus. "Care to dance? Well... Again... If you are not too tired of the short dance earlier?"

Magnus took his hand and got up, one hand holding Alec's hand, and the other over his waist as they moved slowly to Backstreet Boys' How Did I Fall in Love with You.

Magnus, who was just slightly shorter than Alec, was looking down for as long as they danced, without looking up at Alec at all.

"Magnus... You can't just ignore your partner when you dance with him..." Alec said.

Slowly, Magnus looked up at him and that was when he saw tears streaming down Magnus' cheeks.

"I... I can never listened to this song without shedding a tear..." Magnus said, sniffling, shaking his head and putting his head down again, not wanting Alec to see him in tear.

"Awww... Look, I've made an angel cry!" Alec chuckled.

Magnus shook his head and smiled. "God Alexander, where did you learn how to say this kinda thing?"

As Magnus looked up at Alec again, he had already closed himself in, captured his mouth and started kissing him, tasting wine and the saltiness of the tears that were left lingering on his lips.

Magnus moved his hands up, gliding his fingers past the ripples of veins on Alec's strong, muscular arm, up to the back of his neck where he could feel his soft, curly hair and kissed him back hard.

The kiss caught fire as Alec pushed Magnus against the wall near the dining table, causing Magnus to gasp in shock as he felt a slight hit on the back of his head and the coldness of the wall against his body. But they continued to kiss passionately, like the rest of the world was a million miles away.

"This is crazy... You are driving me crazy..." Magnus said, panting a little, as he broke the kiss but hands still holding so tight onto Alec's neck like he was going to die if he ever let go of him, laying their foreheads together.

Alec did not say a word, he grabbed Magnus' ass and scooped him up and moved them few steps away into his room and threw him onto his bed.

"Well at least now we have bigger bed," Alec smirked as he threw himself over Magnus and continue to kiss him, reaching his hands down to pull Magnus pants down, touching him, making him moaned and arched his back in response.

Magnus sat himself up, pushing Alec up as he was sitting on his lap, they undressed themselves within a speed of lightning.

As soon as he saw Alec's bare chests, he immediately put his fingers over Alec's Olympics logo tattoo, caressing it gently, "I've missed this, I've miss you so much..."

"I miss you more Magnus..." Alec said, as he pushed him down onto the bed again, grabbed both his hands as they slid up over his head over the bed sheet, kissing and licking him on his neck, making Magnus moaned in excitement.

The made love, like they had never before. Everything felt

so familiar - the kisses, the movements, the feeling of touching and inside each other's body again like that; yet every time they made love it felt fresh. But this time, it was different, perhaps this was the fresh start they have always been looking forward to.

Chapter 19

April 2019, New York City

Night was settling outside in New York City when Alec and Magnus woke up from their nap to some noisy siren that was wailing from the street.

Magnus stayed snuggling himself in Alec's arms, feeling his chest rising up and down. "Alexander... This is a mistake," Magnus whispered.

"What???" Alec chuckled. "A wise man once told me this isn't what you're supposed to say after sex," Alec was clearly referring to Magnus himself.

"It is a mistake... You have a girlfriend, this isn't right, I don't want to be the third-wheeler, and definitely don't want to be your ex with benefits," Magnus said.

"Well I'm sorry to disappoint you Magnus, but you are not any of those..." Alec said, as he planted a kiss on Magnus' head. "And do you think I'm that kind of guy who would go out with two people at the same time?"

Alec sighed and continued. "I did something really terrible... I broke up with Lydia over text message but you know, me and her, we never really had real feelings for each other anyway..." Magnus could feel Alec shrugging slightly.

Magnus stayed quiet, waiting to hear more from Alec.

"Nothing felt more terrible than seeing you around me yet cannot be with you for real... I was being stupid and I wanted to fix this."

Magnus then got himself up, leaned on his elbows and looked at Alec, caressing his cheekbones lovingly with his fingers. "Me too... It felt so so bad not being able to tell you I love you or I miss you when I really do..." He said with a smile.

"I love you too Magnus," Alec said, taking Magnus' hand from his face and kiss it. "Just give me some time, I'll come out to everyone... I just need to have a chat with my agent, you know to him everything needs planning and stuff..."

"Oh... Does that mean I can include you in my Pride Month column? Olympian Alexander Lightwood's Inspirational Coming Out Story..." Magnus said, like he was reading out the headline of the news.

"But can you promise you won't be bias in the writing though?" Alec chuckled.

"Now that's going to be tough."

They both giggled as Magnus laid back onto the bed.

"I do still have a favour to ask you though, Magnus..."

Magnus turned his face over to face Alec. "What is it?"

"Remember you said whenever I need you, you will always be there?"

"Of course, even if I'm not physically there..."

"Yes, but this time you will have to be physically there."

Magnus looked at Alec with confusion all over his face but he knew, whatever it was going to be, he will be keeping his promise and be there for him.

Chapter 20

April 2016, Perth, Western Australia

It was another rainy Autumn evening as Magnus hopped off the bus, arriving back at his apartment from a late meeting with the Indonesian Students Society.

He had to run towards the apartment building in the rain but as he was approaching the building, he saw a tall figure standing outside right next to the entrance; one hand holding a small box, another with a backpack on, body soaking wet and shivering in the cold. He couldn't believe his eyes when he realised it was Alec.

"Oh my god Alec, what are you doing here?" He asked, tilting his chin up with his hand to have a better look at him.

"It's your birthday... I bought you cake."

"Why didn't you call me first? Come on..." Magnus said as he opened the door into the building and pulled Alec in.

"I... I wanted to surprise you..." Alec said with a trembling voice.

As they went up, Magnus has gotten Alec to take a shower, made him a hot chocolate as they sat on his bed.

"Happy Birthday Magnus..." Alec said, as Magnus took a spoonful of the cake he had bought for him.

"You silly boy, I don't even like cakes! But I'm eating it all because... Because you are silly enough to do such silly thing for me... Thank you..." Magnus said as he gave Alec a peck on his cheek, leaving icing on it.

Magnus smiled and went on to lick the icing off his face.

"I have a gift for you..." Alec got up and reached for his wet backpack and took out a little box. "Here..."

Magnus opened the box and found a silver lapel pin that came in shape of letters 'MB' on it.

"Thank you Alexander..." He paused. "You know what, I should give you something back too..."

Alec watched as Magnus opened the second drawer of his desk and took out a small book, reached for a pen lying on the desk, turned a few first pages, and started writing something on it before passing it to Alec.

"I just got this the other day, I wanted to keep it for myself but I can get another one..." Magnus shrugged.

It was The Catcher in the Rye, the book that meant so much to them. Alec flipped opened the book to the second page where there was a blank page and saw the writing that Magnus left.

'Dear Alexander,

Aku Cinta Kamu!

Your Magnus'

"Aku cinta kamu?" Alec asked.

"That's Indonesian for I love you," Magnus smiled.

That made Alec all giddy up as he returned the smile. "Aku cinta kamu," he repeated softly.

Magnus went on to kiss him on his lips, cupping his cheeks with both his hands, before letting them go almost immediately.

"Gosh Alec, your face is hot!" He said as he reached his hand to touch his forehand. "You are having a fever... It must be the rain..." Magnus looked extremely concerned.

"Yeah I'm starting to feel a little dizzy actually..." Alec said.

"Lie down Alec, please."

Alec obliged and decided to rest on Magnus' bed. He watched as Magnus frantically put the gifts and the cake on the desk, cover him with his blanket and was leaving the bed to go somewhere. He reached out and grabbed his wrist. "Don't leave me Magnus," he said, weakly.

Magnus bend down by his side, brushing his forehead gently. "Silly boy, I'm not going anywhere, I'll always be there for you, even if I'm not physically there." He looked at Alec lovingly and continued. "But I have to go get you a cold towel, and check if my housemate has any paracetamol... I'll be back in a minute," he said, planting a kiss on his forehead.

As Magnus rushed out of the room, he couldn't help but shook his head, wondering if he was doing the right thing, if Alec was right about the relationship being a mistake. It hurt to see Alec being so nice to him and he doesn't know if he was worth all that love and attention, and then to see all of it die when he will be packing his bags and leaving Alec soon.

But he was determined to keep the promise to him, that he will be there for him. He hoped Alec will know and remember that he will always be there for him, even if they might be far apart from each other.

Chapter 21

May 2019, New York City

Throughout the times that Alec had known Magnus, he was always unapologetically him - be it the way he talks, the way he dresses or the fact that he was so out and proud. He was always the confident one, the positive one, and the one who gave him the most motivations whenever he needed them.

So it came as such a great surprise to see him looking so extremely nervous, hands shaking and all worried about how he looked for the occasion. He certainly did not expect Magnus to be so anxious when he asked him to come along to his family lunch so that he can officially come out to his them.

As they stood outside the Lightwoods' house, Magnus couldn't help but asked, "Okay, is my shirt wrinkly?"

Alec chuckled. "It's fine! And that's like the 50th times you've asked me today!"

"My hair? How does it look? I'm having a stomachache like

suddenly, I'm too nervous to do this... What if they hate your coming out and hate me?"

"Magnus... You look perfect, as always, and even if they hate my coming out, I'm pretty sure they will love you," Alec smiled, and edged in to give him a peck on his cheek. "If anything, I should be more nervous than you but you looking cute as hell like this... I think I'm feeling better," Alec beamed and proceeded to open the door as the two of them walked into the house.

"Hey you are here!" Isabelle came welcoming them, giving Alec a hug.

Their mother Maryse who was trailing behind her, also proceeded to hug Alec but paused when she saw Magnus standing next to him. "And this is?" Maryse eyed over Isabelle and Alec, hoping to get an answer.

"Magnus, Magnus Bane, nice to meet you... I've got us some wine!" Magnus said, reaching a hand out to shake Maryse and Isabelle's hands, the other wiggling the bottle of wine in the air.

As they moved inside, Isabelle had given her brother a questioning stare but Alec simply shrugged it off.

As they sat down on the dining table, Robert came out from his room and was formally introduced to Magnus. As soon as Magnus told Robert where he worked at, Robert went all excited telling him he was a fan of the weekly magazine, much to Magnus' surprise, as he always thought the magazine was small and no one really bothered reading it.

They hit it off right away, chit-chatting about all the current affairs that was going on in the world and within the city.

Alec, who was most concerned about his father's reaction was secretly pleased to see them getting along so well despite only meeting for the first time.

As everyone was settled at the table, Alec started squeezing Magnus' hand under the table out of nervousness as he prepared himself for the worst. But with Magnus sitting besides him, he knew he was ready. In fact, he never felt as ready as now.

"Okay... I have any announcement to make..." It was Isabelle who started the conversation before any food on the table was attacked.

"Simon proposed!" She exclaimed, flashing a ring on her ring finger to everyone.

Like a balloon loosing its air, Alec sat flustered and couldn't believe what just happened. This was supposed to be a big moment, possibly the biggest moment in his life and he had rehearsed the short speech for a million times before coming home. And now suddenly he had lost the moment and did not know what to do.

His mind went blank when his parents got up from their seats and went to hug his sister, congratulating her. Seconds later, he saw Magnus doing the same too so he quickly did the same, but everything felt so blur to him in the end.

It was Magnus who finally brought him back to senses when he felt his hand stroking his lap under the table. He looked up at Magnus as he gave him a smile and nod.

"It's okay... Later..." He could read Magnus lips as he uttered those words out silently.

Chapter 22

May 2019, New York City

After lunch, Alec was helping Maryse with the dishes in the kitchen when he couldn't wait any longer to tell his mother what he had been wanting to tell her.

"Mom, what do you think of Magnus?" He asked.

"He's charming... You know Alec, it would be nice if you could pre-empt me next time if you are bringing a friend. You know how worry I was that we didn't have enough food?"

"Oh Magnus isn't a big eater... And he is not my friend mom..." Alec paused and took a long deep breath. "He's ah... We are seeing each other."

There was a silent gasp from Maryse as she turned to look at Alec in shock, making Alec feeling a little uncomfortable.

"I'm sorry mom... I'm gay..."

This time Maryse blinked in surprise. "Oh don't be sorry, you have nothing to be sorry about..." She cleaned her hands and took her son in and hugged him. "I'm not some old-fashioned conservative mom... I've just been wondering why you never brought Lydia home... Now I know..."

This was when Isabelle came out of nowhere and joined the hug. "Urggghhh... I'm so proud of you, Alec! Finally!" She said.

Alec let out a sigh of relief as he turned and looked at Isabelle with a raised eyebrow. "What do you mean finally?"

"You were never interested with any of my friends! And my friends are always the best-looking ones and were literally flashing their cleavages when they were around you but you never gave them the attention they wanted!" Isabelle shrugged.

Alec knew indeed that his sister knew him best.

"Alec, gay or straight, you are still my boy and nothing is going to change the love I have for you..." Maryse said, squeezing both his arms.

Alec felt a lump at the back of his throat listening to his mother's words.

"And... Looks like he is good with your dad..." She added as they peeked at Magnus and Robert still chit-chatting and laughing in the living room.

"And he is cute..." Isabelle elbowed his brother and grinned.

Moments later, when they were done in the kitchen, Alec found Magnus in his old room, holding the book that he had gifted to him three years ago.

He went behind Magnus, wrapped his arms around his waist and rested his chin on his shoulder. "Aku Cinta Kamu... I always remember that..." He whispered.

Magnus smiled and asked, "Is everything okay in the kitchen?"

"Yeah... And thank you."

Magnus turned himself around to face Alec, laying both his hands over the back of his neck as he stared into his eye lovingly. "For?"

"For being here... I don't know what to do without you around me..."

"Well... It's been a pleasure Mr. Lightwood..." He replied and gave Alec a little peck on his lips.

This was when Alec's phone kept ringing with text messages coming in.

"Go check your messages," Magnus ordered.

Alec walked away and took out his phone. The first few messages were pictures of him and Magnus at the cafe the other day - them talking at their table, them dancing and even one with him cleaning Magnus' mouth with a serviette. Then came messages from Valentine.

"Wtf Alec? Is this why you broke up with Lydia???"

Chapter 23

May 2019, New York City

Magnus' article where he wrote about the interview with
the film director just gotten praises from his editor Luke at
their weekly meeting. It got him all pumped-up for more
good articles to be featured in his Pride Month column,
which would mean so much to him when they finally go to
print.

As the team wrapped up their meeting, he jogged back to
his desk and was eager to start writing and planning for
his next article when Clary came sitting herself on his desk
right next to his computer.

"Magnus... This is insane!" She said.

"What's insane?" Magnus asked, eyes still glued to the
computer monitor without looking back at her.

"Your plan to go interview this group of homophobic
people!"

He turned and laid himself on the back of his chair,

crossed his arms and looked up at Clary. "Why is it insane? I think it's only fair we talk to them and listen to why they are doing what they are doing!"

"These people are crazy! More than just protesting and making stupid statements, they sometimes attack gay people... Like you!"

"Oh I'll be fine..." Magnus rolled his eyes.

"Don't tell them you are gay..." Clary said with a determined voice.

"Out of question." Magnus replied, very firmly.

"Then let me go with you, why am I not included in this assignment?"

"Because... They don't want to be pictured! You are not needed!"

Clary crossed her arms and stood up. "I just don't have a very good feeling about this..."

"My dear biscuit, I'll be fine, I promise, I will take care of myself and I'll nudge you guys if anything happen, don't worry," Magnus held Clary's hands and pulled her down as she sat down again on his desk.

"At least give me an emergency contact... Maybe your

mom back home?"

"You and Raphael are my closest friends here so there, you, my emergency contact," Magnus snorted. "And don't you dare contacting my mom until... Until I'm dead..." Magnus paused, suddenly feeling the fear for his mother receiving a phone call to tell her that her son is dead.

"There must be someone else?" Clary asked.

This was when Magnus started scribbling down two phone numbers on a piece of paper and passed it over to Clary.

"Here, one's my mom in Indonesia, one's... I don't think so you will need any of it but there you go..." Magnus said.

"Hey breaking news!" Raphael cut into the conversation, hand holding his phone. "Lydia Branwell is engaged! To Alexander Lightwood!" He screamed.

The words came like a million pieces of needles piercing through Magnus' heart as he quickly grabbed Raphael's phone to see a picture Lydia posted on her Instagram. It was her hand with a huge diamond ring on her ring finger, captioned 'I said yes!'.

It was a picture without Alec in it. But he did not need to be - he was tagged in the picture so it was understood who she was engaged to.

"Urggghhh... Another hot guy taken..." Clary sighed.

Chapter 24

May 2019, New York City

Alec sat at the far end corner of the pub, with a cap on his head, and had kept his head low, staring into the glass of beer he was holding in his hand.

He had been waiting for a good 15 minutes for Magnus to appear. He wondered if he would ever appear.

Then the door flung open and he saw a tall figure walking in, also with a cap on him, looking around carefully, as though to make sure nobody was following him. The door slammed behind him as he walked further in and saw Alec.

He looked up and gave him a nod as he walked towards him at the table and sat himself down.

"Magnus... It wasn't me... My agent Valentine and Lydia set me up..." Alec said, making sure his head wasn't looking too high up and that he wasn't too loud.

"I know Alec, I know... I know you too well and I know how the industry works as well..." Magnus said.

"I'm sorry Magnus..."

"It's not exactly your fault..." Magnus sighed helplessly.

There was a long, mournful silence.

"Alec, I came back to New York for the freedom to write, freedom to be myself and freedom to love; not like how I am now... I mean, look at us two looking ridiculous as fuck in caps and don't even dare looking up at each other..." Magnus shook his head as he spoke.

"Magnus... I can come out, I have to, I have to tell people the truth..." Alec said.

"No Alexander..." Magnus paused and looked around cautiously. "At least not now... One moment you are engaged to your girlfriend, next moment you break the engagement... I don't think that will do any good to your image or your career."

"Then..."

"I love you Alexander..." Magnus reached his hand out to hold Alec's, but there was so much doubt in his expression as he looked at him blankly. "But I think you need to figure out what to do next, what do you really want from your career, from your stupid agent and I need to figure out what I really want out of this..."

"Perhaps, we shouldn't be doing anything yet... Your Olympics qualifying event is coming soon and that should be the priority, not you and me..."

"Are you... Breaking up with me?" Alec could feel the fear in the words he just uttered.

"Were we officially together in the first place? It was all a mistake... We should have let you settle everything before we get back together..."

Alec looked up at Magnus properly for the very first time since he sat down. It was hard to describe how he looked like as his face was covered with heavy shadow from the cap he was wearing but it was obvious there was an air of grief, or perhaps disappointment on his face.

"I guess we can say we need a break?" Magnus shrugged.

"Like Rachel and Ross in Friends?" Alec couldn't believe he could find the courage to actually chuckle a little.

"Like Rachel and Ross..." Magnus paused for a second and continued. "Look, it'll be nice to stay away from each other and all these dramas for a while so you can focus on your competition... Just remember, I'll always be there for you, no matter how far away I am, okay?" And with that, Magnus stood up, patted Alec on his shoulder and walked out of the pub.

Chapter 25

As the next Olympics qualifying event drew closer, Alec had been training harder, extending the hours of training, hoping that all these effort is enough for his first and probably last Olympics appearance.

As he returned to his apartment alone after another long day at the pool, he threw himself onto the couch exhausted, trying to figure out what he wanted for dinner tonight before calling for food delivery.

Few days had past since the engagement announcement that Valentine and Lydia had set him up with. At the beginning, there were a few phone calls asking for his comments, which he politely passed to Valentine to handle, then it all died down.

To his own surprise, nobody really bothered asking him anymore details. All people were concerned about was what is Lydia going to wear at the wedding, which designers was she looking at... The paparazzi seemed to be following her around town just to get the answers, rather than him.

The news had left his family confused since they had just been introduced to Magnus and embraced his coming out a while ago. His teammates were all congratulating him but he did not give a shit about any of them.

From being angry to being helpless, he had no idea what his next step should be. He wanted so badly to come out to the public and tell everyone all that he had with Lydia were just marketing gimmick. But Magnus was right, that might do more harm to his image and his career than anything else.

He hadn't seen or heard from Magnus too for a few days now. He wondered how was he doing? Does he want to talk to him? If he text him now, will he reply his message?

He was deep in his thought when his phone rang. An unknown number appeared on the screen and he hesitated whether to answer it. He certainly did not want to answer a call from any of the reporters wanting to know details of his relationship with Lydia which he had no idea what was right to tell.

The ringing stopped after a while.

Then it rang again. This time he took it.

"Hello?"

"Hello? Urm... I don't know who are you but I'm Clary, I'm Magnus' colleague... You do know Magnus right? Cos he gave me your number as emergency contact," Clary said on the other end of the phone.

"Yes?" Alec answered, but with a doubtful tone, wondering what was the call all about.

"Okay... Magnus had gone to interview a group of very loud homophobic people yesterday. These people are notorious and I tried to stop him but he didn't want to listen..." Clary paused and let out a sigh. "He went off yesterday and hasn't return to work today and it's already night time now..."

"What? Did you try calling him?"

"Of course we did! His phone is already turned off, we've gone to his apartment too but no one was there... And we are starting to worry... Anyway, if he contact you please, please let me know, and I'll update you when we hear anything from him."

As soon as he hung up, Alec could feel his stomach churning.

It sounded so typical of Magnus - he remembered vividly that he had once told him that certain things were worth fighting for, including gay rights and equalities. But was it worth risking his life for, really?

Then a horrifying thought gripped his mind... He thought about all the crime stories that Magnus had told him about when he was doing research for his assignment back in Perth where there were cases gays were sexually tortured, beaten and left to die in some deserted places. Surely Magnus wouldn't become one of the numbers, right?

The thought of Magnus being tortured, or even dying kept crawling into his head, as he kept looking for news updates on his phone, and found it hard to go through the night without worrying and panicking.

He hardly had enough of sleep but the next thing he knew, his alarm rang and he had to wake up to go for his training.

It was after he had parked his car outside the pool that he got a message from Clary.

"We found him!"

Chapter 26

March 2016, Perth, Western Australia

As the very last heat of summer burned off to make way for autumn, the city of Perth was looking stunning with red and yellow painted all over the streets.

Magnus had taken Alec on their first date at a quaint little suburban cafe. Sitting themselves at the high table by the side of the ceiling-to-floor glass window, facing outside, they were enjoying their coffee and brunch as well as the beautiful view as the sun shone onto them through the glass.

Alec was still very shy and quiet so Magnus was eager to get him to feel more comfortable around him.

"How's your coffee?" Magnus asked.

"Urm... It's alright I guess... I mean, I don't know much about coffee actually..." Alec shrugged.

"You will know eventually, coffee is huge here and it's a shame you have lactose intolerance because when in

Australia, you have Flat White!" Magnus said as he raised his cup of coffee and took a sip.

Awkward silence.

"So Alexander... Tell me which style do you do?" Magnus asked, with one hand cupping his own chin, turning himself to look at Alec.

"Huh? What?"

"I mean... Freestyle? Breaststroke? Backstroke? Butterfly?"

"Oh... Urm... Recently my new coach in UC had pushed me to be more into Backstroke, it's less competitive in the States, apparently..." Alec shrugged.

"Backstroke! I always find it amazing how people can do that in a straight line without looking! I mean if I were to compete in the next lane to you I'll most probably swim out of my lane and hit you first thing!"

That statement made Alec laugh while shaking his head in disbelief. "I don't know... Maybe it's an instinct thing?" He said, still wearing a smile on his face as he spoke.

"I really like it when you smile or laugh like this, you should do that more," Magnus said, eyes staring at him in adoration, making Alec flushed instantly.

"I'm going to look for a 50m pool here so you can start training and get you into the next Olympics," Magnus said, sounding very determined.

Alec looked stunned hearing that. "Why?"

"Why? Isn't Olympic Games every athlete's dream?"

"Then what is your dream? Do you wanna do something like war journalism? What is the highest award they give to a journalist?" Alec asked.

"War zone journalist?" Magnus chuckled. "Even if I had dreamt of becoming a war zone journalist, I would have totally changed my mind after watching movies like Saving Private Ryan! I don't want my head to be blew up like that! Poof!!!" He said as he did his hand gestures over his head. "I want to die pretty, okay!"

A vain pot Magnus had managed to make Alec smile again.

"I don't know actually, I just want to do things that change people's lives you know, or change people's perceptions on certain subjects, and trust me, a journalistic award is harder to get compared to an Olympic gold medal..." He paused. "But some things are worth fighting for, even if it means there might be no material rewards."

"Like?"

"I don't know?" Magnus shrugged. "Like equality, gay rights, an Olympic Games outing even if you might not win any medal in the end... And you..." Magnus smiled, looking at Alec.

"Me? Even for only six months?" Alec asked.

"Yes... Even for only six month..."

Alec couldn't help but reached out to Magnus' hand under the table and let their fingers interlocked - the first time they held hands like that; then rested his head on Magnus' shoulder - also the first time he did that in full view of the public.

Magnus then planted a kiss on Alec's head. "Just promise me, don't be afraid, don't let this injury affect you, you gotta fight this and I'm going to help you as much as I can."

Alec nodded lightly as Magnus wrapped him in his arms lovingly as they took in the beautiful ambience of their first date.

Chapter 27

May 2019, New York City

When Alec arrived at the hospital, Clary was already sitting outside the room with Raphael. He recognised Raphael straight away and jogged quickly towards them.

"Urm... Hi..." He said, still panting slightly from the rush to the hospital.

The pair looked up and were obviously surprised to see him towering over them.

"Alexander Lightwood? You are Magnus' emergency contact?" Clary looked dumbfounded and turned to Raphael for assurance.

Raphael gave her a tiny nod.

"Yeah... I guess? We... We are good friends," Alec stammered a little, struggling to find the right words to describe his relationship with Magnus. "How is he?"

"We found him outside our office building this morning...

He was unconscious and quite sure with a broken leg...
And ahhh... He just doesn't look too good..." Raphael
explained.

Alec could see both Clary and Raphael looked extremely
worried and it made him wondered how bad were the
injuries Magnus had suffered and couldn't stop imagining
what had those assholes done to him.

Few seconds later, a doctor in charge and a few medical
staffs came out of the room.

"Doctor! How is he?" Clary asked, grabbing the doctor's
arm.

"Mr. Bane... He was badly-dehydrated, suffered quite a
number of bruises and cuts all over his body, and a broken
leg..."

"Is he... Sexually assaulted?" Alec blurted.

"Fortunately, no sign of sexual abuse but... It looks like we
will have to keep him in the ICU for now," said the doctor,
looking a little worried.

"What? Why? What do you mean?" Alec asked, concerned.

"He is having a high fever, most probably from a swollen
kidney. We believe there were severe kicking and punching
both on his abdominal and lower back that caused his

kidney to swell." The doctor paused and the three of them could see his face changed. "This means he could either suffer a kidney infection, which is not life-threatening, or not yet; or it could cause internal bleeding, and among other things... Death."

"Death? No no no no... You have to save him," Alec begged.

"We will try, that is why we will have to observe him in the ICU until the fever subside and run tests. Until then, we can only hope that he won't slip away..."

As the doctor left, Alec, Clary and Raphael walked cautiously into the room to see Magnus.

Alec's could hear his heart shattered into million pieces when he saw Magnus lying lifelessly on the bed. His right leg was all wrapped up in a cement bandage, his left eye was extremely swollen and there were small cut wounds all over his pale face. But it was all the confusing tubes attached to his body and connecting to all the medical machines that broke his heart the most.

Clary was already in tears as Raphael took her in and comforted her, stroking her arm lightly. Alec felt like he needed that hug too as he couldn't believe what he was seeing, but he resisted and tried to calm himself down, holding back tears that were welling up in his eyes.

Later, he had told Clary and Raphael to go back to work, as he had taken the day off to stay in the hospital.

He took a seat next to the bed, having a closer look at Magnus now - hair all ruined, face so pale and lips so dry he wondered how long hadn't Magnus drink or eat anything. Even his non-swollen eye had dark shadow under it he wondered if he had been kept awake all the while by those assholes.

And with so many tiny cuts on his face he knew Magnus would be so mad when he sees himself like that. He touched his cheek with the back of his fingers and felt the heat from the fever he was having and couldn't help but be worried for him.

He then took Magnus' hand and placed it near his lips and kissed it gently. "Magnus... It's me, Alec, I'm here..." He said, as he found himself choking to his own words. "I can't... I can't see you looking like this Magnus... But that's alright as long as you wake up and be okay..."

"I love you so much you'd have no idea... So please, please don't die on me..." Alec finally uttered the words that he was so desperate to say to Magnus, and they were words that were enough for him to break down in tears.

But like how Magnus had always manage to make him one, he knew Magnus was a fighter. He will fight for his life.

Chapter 28

May 2019, New York City

Alec hadn't skip any of his days of training, but had also without fail, checking-in the hospital every night to be with Magnus, whose temperature was still unstable and was still unconscious.

But it was comforting to be by his side - sometimes talking to him but most times just listening to him inhaling and exhaling heavily through the heartbeat monitor, telling him that he was well alive.

It was the fourth night after he wrapped up his training, had a quick dinner and arrived at Magnus' room in the hospital.

His heart skipped a beat when he saw the bed empty and everything else in the room was all cleared off.

What happened to Magnus?

Is Magnus gone?

He felt himself fumbling a few steps backwards and
bumped into someone behind him.

"Sir, are you family member of Mr. Bane?" It was a nurse
whom he had bumped into.

"Yes... What happened to him?"

"Oh, his fever is gone and he had regained consciousness
so we cleared him to be transferred to a normal room up
on level three," she said with a smile.

He sped off right away and as he arrived at the room, he
saw Magnus sitting just slightly up on his bed, struggling
to reach his hand out to grab the glass laying on the side
table. He breathed an air of relief and couldn't help but
smiled as he walked into the room.

"Let me help you with that," he said.

"Oh Alexander, you're my saviour! I'm so freaking thirsty,"
Magnus cried out.

Alec took the glass of water and held it as Magnus took a
few sips of water but soon started coughing, choking on
the water.

"Slowly..." Alec said, stroking his shoulder gently.

"Mmm... Thank you..." Magnus said, as he leaned himself

back on the bed, wincing slightly in pain.

"Are you feeling alright?"

"No... I feel like I've been ran over by a bus... No, correction... At least 20 busses..." Magnus grimaced.

Alec was smiling in joy as he sat down on the chair next to the bed. "I'm just so glad you are okay..."

"Oh I have to be okay or those bastards will run free for what they have put me through!" Magnus growled.

"Hey hey, take it easy... You really gave everyone a scare you know? Do you know how worried I was?"

"I know, they told me a tall, handsome guy was with me every night without fail and I don't know anybody but you who is tall and handsome... I'm just surprised they don't recognise you!"

Alec shrugged. "Well I'm not as famous as you thought I guess?"

"You are going to be... Oh shit, what day is it today? Did you miss the qualifying event already?"

"No... I'm flying off in another two days time..."

"Phew..." Magnus let out a sigh of relief.

Alec reached his hand out to caress Magnus cheek, very carefully, making sure he doesn't touch any of the cut wounds.

"Magnus, the past few days had been a real torture... The thought of losing you forever almost break me..." Alec paused for a bit, realising Magnus' had been staring at him lovingly. "I love you Magnus, and I don't want to live my life without you, really... So please just let me be with you."

Magnus raised a smile sweetly listening to Alec. He grabbed Alec's hand from his face and held it tight. "I love you too, Alexander... You know when those assholes started beating me up, I wasn't afraid of them at all, I was pretty much prepared for the worst. But then every single time I thought about you and about not being able to see you again, I told myself that I have to survive that, I have to fight my way back to you."

"We have wasted so much time in between and I'm not going to let anything come between us anymore." Magnus added.

Alec beamed and stood up, leaned down and gave Magnus a peck on his lips. He could feel Magnus' lips curled up in a smile while kissing him back.

"But as much as I want you by my side all the time, I also want you to go all out for the Olympics. Promise me this time around you will make it so I can travel with you to

Tokyo next year, okay?"

"I promise," Alec said, with a smile.

"Go get em' tiger!"

Chapter 29

June 2019, Busan, South Korea

"I'm feeling much better Alexander, the antibiotic is working well on the infection and I don't feel the pain so much now, don't you worry about me..."

"I'm so glad you're better, you should rest more, I mean, what time is it there in New York?"

Magnus chuckled on the other side of the phone. "It's very early... But I'm not going to miss seeing my love swimming in one of the most important races in his life!"

Alec could hear some noises coming from the back, some people fake-gagging or something like that, followed by a lot of giggling, he knew it was Clary and Raphael fooling around in Magnus' room.

"I'm sorry... Clary and Raphael are way too single to understand this..." Magnus said. "Ouch! My foot!"

"Okay okay, I really need to go now..." Alec said in a hurried tone.

"Okay... Well, break a leg! And I love you!!! Muaks muaks muaks!"

"Love you too! Muaks!"

Alec had a huge smile on his face as he hung up the phone. His heart was definitely full knowing that Magnus is healthy and happy and that they are now back together and nobody could stop them anymore.

He had already hunt down his first Olympics ticket two days ago in the 200m backstroke event and was going out for a second one in the 100m event.

He followed the event officials out, stood right at the starting line and prepared for the race.

He had his swimming cap on, goggles on, flexed his muscles, swung his arms to warm up a little. As the official introduced the swimmers one by one, he made sure he looked up at the camera when it was his turn. He flashed a sweet smile at the camera - something he doesn't normally do, but he did it knowing that Magnus was watching from home.

A whistle blew off and Alec and the other swimmers jumped straight into the water, took their position holding the bar at the side of the pool, curled themselves up at the starting line - a practice for all backstroke events.

Then the buzzer went off and all the swimmers got off almost simultaneously.

Alec's strokes were strong and confident, but not overly fast yet - his strategy was to save all his strength and energy to the final 50m.

With every stroke he made, he thought about how just three years ago, he was forced to give up fighting for an Olympic Games entry due to an injury and it was enough to crush his confidence he wanted to quit swimming entirely. Then he met Magnus, whom despite not a swimmer himself, or a sportsman, had taught him to be courages, to be resilient and to chase his dream once more.

Magnus had made him a better person and was one of the reasons he felt alive again in his swimming career. He was glad that he was there for him as he swam into the Olympic Games, although not physically.

He was swimming for himself and his childhood dream, but he was also more determined than ever to swim for Magnus as a reward for all the love, supports and encouragements, even prayers that he had had for him over the years.

He could hear cheers coming from the crowd of spectators as he swam and finished the first 50m and made a perfect turn. He did not know, and would not know how fast he was or in which position until the end of the race so all he

could do now was to swim his heart out, until he feel
exhausted, until he could touch the side of the pool again.

You've got this, he thought to himself.

Chapter 30

June 2019, New York City

It was very early on a Saturday morning in New York City as Clary and Raphael gathered in Magnus' room in the hospital, chomping down breakfast and sipping their morning coffee that they have bought some for Magnus too.

Magnus had by now told them about Alec and being his best friends, they have decided to accompany him as they watched him on television live, fighting for another ticket to the Olympic Games.

When Alec appeared on the TV for the first time as he was introduced, Magnus was so excited he let out a growl. "Go Alec! Go... Ouch..." Magnus winced a little, feeling the pain coming from his body that is still recovering from all the bruises and cuts.

"Hey careful you... Calm down, he hasn't even started swimming yet!" Clary laughed.

They looked on as Alec took his position in the pool.

It was the 100m backstroke event - Alec's pet event so
Magnus had some confidence in Alec making it but before
the swim is over, nobody knows what was going to happen.
He needed to finish the race in top three to automatically
qualify for the Olympics and Magnus was literally biting
his teeth and all tensed up feeling nervous as hell for Alec.

Then off he swam, as fast as he could. He was in third
position after the first lap and they could see him stroking
harder and much faster from there on, passing the
swimmer who was in the second place at first. Then almost
at the final 10m Alec made his big move, swimming even
faster and got himself closer to the leader as they touched
the side of the pool to finish the race, almost looking like
they have wrapped the race up at the same time.

The two swimmers looked up at the result board, which
now showed Alec had won the race with his best time yet.
He punched his fists into the air in celebration of the
victory.

"He's done it! The oldest member of the U.S. swim team,
Alexander Lightwood had done it! Making his debut
Olympics next year in not one, but two events!" The
commentator said, almost sounded like he was yelling in
excitement.

"Yasssss!!!" Magnus, Clary and Raphael screamed in the
room, then giving each other high fives.

"Oh god... I'm so proud!" Magnus was beaming from ear-to-ear.

"Look at you, I've never seen you like this before!" Clary chuckled.

"Oh I think we can expect more of this in the future..." Raphael teased.

Magnus rolled his eyes but couldn't hide his happiness and pride in that smile he was wearing. He had never felt so proud of someone he knew in his entire life.

"Okay, okay... Here comes the interview... Shhhh..." Clary said.

The three of them shifted their attentions to the TV again as they heard the American journalist started asking Alec, who had just came out of the pool, cap off, goggle off, water still dripping out of his hair, but looking extremely overjoyed.

"How do you feel Alec, another place in the Olympics!"

"I'm honestly ecstatic, you know, I've worked very hard for this and I'm just glad all the hard work had finally paid off..." Alec said, still panting from the swim, and probably from the excitement.

"Anything you want to say to your friends and family back

home? Or to your fiancé Lydia?"

The question caused Magnus, Clary and Raphael to cringe a little. An utter air of awkwardness filled the room as they waited for Alec's response to the question.

They saw Alec took just a few seconds to gather himself, he swallowed and said, "Yeah... I do actually have something to say..." Alec paused for a little bit. "I'm gay, I've always been gay... And I'm in love with a man, he is the love of my life and I wouldn't be able to do any of this without him, his love and support."

There was a silence from the TV.

Magnus, Clary and Raphael were now as shocked as the journalist who was clearly too surprised and did not know how to continue the interview.

Then Alec started to talk again. "I'm coming back to you, baby," he said, winked at the camera, then walked away, leaving the stunned journalist, who was still struggling to find words to say.

Clary and Raphael with jaw hanging, turned to look at Magnus who was also looking as shock as them.

"I swear I know nothing about this!" He said, holding his hands up.

Finale

June 2019, New York City

The arrival hall at the John F. Kennedy International
Airport was experiencing its usual busy, crowded day with
countless passengers arriving. Some of them arrived
without anybody welcoming them and would hail a cab to
leave the airport, some would arrived to warm hugs and
kisses.

On this day though, there was a small crowd of media,
mostly sport journalists, photographers and camera crews
standing by waiting for Alec's return from South Korea.

Alec finally securing his place in next year's Olympics
wasn't really quite a big deal to a nation that has always
been one of the powerhouses in swimming event, but his
surprise coming out had definitely made headlines,
shocking some of the people in both the sports and
entertainment industries, even his own teammates.

He did not really know what he had gotten himself into but
he knew Valentine wasn't happy about it and had threaten
him about him violating their contract. But he was relieved

and glad that he had finally done that and no Valentine nor Lydia could stop him anymore, he thought.

As he walked out of the arrival hall, pulling his only luggage behind him, camera flashes almost blinded his eyes as he squinted to the sudden attention aiming at him.

He was taken aback and stood frozen as he did not know how to respond. He had never been bombarded by such a huge crowd of people his entire life.

This was when he saw his family - Robert, Maryse and Isabelle came running to him, hugging him and congratulating him. He briefly heard them saying words like "I'm so proud of you" and "well done Alec" before they started leading him through the crowd but the group of journalists and cameras wouldn't stop following them until they paused half way through the crowd.

"We have a surprise for you Alec!" Isabelle grinned.

"Alexander!"

He heard a familiar voice shouting out his name and looked straight to where the voice came from and saw him.

There stood Magnus, the man he had fell so madly in love with, looking much better now without the swollen eye. He could see he made an effort to look good - hair properly-styled and dressed well for the occasion, but his broken leg still in a bandage, holding onto crutches with both his arms, Clary and Raphael by his side, all smiling and helping him to balance in those crutches.

The Lightwoods were all smiled too by now.

"What are you waiting for?" Isabelle asked, while elbowing her brother.

He ran towards Magnus, as Magnus too, limped his way out to him as fast as he could in those crutches. When they got closer, Magnus let go of his crutches as they flung off, falling off almost like in a slow-motion mode, onto the ground; and threw himself off freely as he stumbled against Alec, knowing for sure Alec was going to catch him as they wrapped each other around with a tight, passionate hug.

"You did it! I'm so so so proud of you Alexander," Magnus said into his ear.

Alec drew himself back, but hands holding onto Magnus' arms, making sure he was supporting him as he stood on one leg, smiled at him and said, "Olympics dream is one thing, but you know, I realised that you, are my real dream come true."

Magnus slid his hands up to clench onto the back Alec's neck, and was beaming from ear-to-ear. "I love you Alexander," he said.

"I love you too," Alec replied, as he closed in, capturing Magnus' mouth and kissed him.

They kissed for as long as they could. They could feel and hear ripples of applause and whistling from the crowd; camera flashing and clicking away behind them but nothing was going to stop them.

As the broke the kiss and looked into each other's eyes, they remembered vividly the last time they kissed so passionately at an airport - a farewell kiss at the Perth International Airport.

This time around though, it was a kiss for a beginning of a brand new journey - a journey they were both so ready to walk down together.